got to dance

M. C. Helldorfer

Pictures by Hiroe Nakata

A Doubleday Book for Young Readers

A Doubleday Book for Young Readers

Published by
Random House Children's Books
a division of
Random House, Inc.
New York

Doubleday and the anchor with dolphin colophon are registered trademarks of
Random House, Inc.

Text copyright © 2004 by M. C. Helldorfer
Illustrations copyright © 2004 by Hiroe Nakata

Visit us on the Web! www.randomhouse.com/kids
Educators and librarians, for a variety of teaching tools, visit us at
www.randomhouse.com/teachers

Library of Congress Cataloging-in-Publication data is available upon request.
ISBN: 0-385-32628-9 (trade)   0-385-90865-2 (lib. bdg.)

The text of this book is set in 41-point Chauncy Deluxxe.

Book design by Trish Parcell Watts

MANUFACTURED IN CHINA

May 2004

10 9 8 7 6 5 4 3 2 1

To Nicholas and Sarah,
with love
—M.C.H.

For my music teacher, Miss Toda
—H.N.

Momma's gone to work,
Brother's gone to camp.
Nothing to do, oh, nothing to do.
Just Grandpa and me—
I've got the summertime blues—
got to dance.

Pancakes are flipping,
old slippers slipping—
got to dance, dance.

Bare feet—yow!—
the burning hot street
makes me dance, dance.

Cold squirting from the hose—
got popsicle toes.
I do a penguin dance.

Sandals slapping,
water smacking:
Look at Grandpa dance!

Two big bowls
of berries rock and roll—
a RAINING-DOWN dance.

Going to the zoo,
see Grandpa's yellow shoes—
every-birdy dance!

Beneath the bus seats,
jig-jigging feet
do a crosstown dance.

Laces tied in knots,
I pull one sneaker off
and hoppity-hop dance.

Clean shirt and socks,
my bed springy soft:
Boing-boing dance.

Shoes with wings,
flying dreams—

whoa!

An upside-down dance.

After my nap,
old shoes with straps—
tap dancing tap tap.

Summer shower and boots,
squishy worms and roots—
my easy oozy dance.

Brother home from camp.
Two hungry bears do
a prowling, growling,
howling dance.

Momma in her slippers
sings and makes us dinner.
Oh, Hamburger Boogie!
I just got to dance—

dancing holes in my socks,
dancing holes in my shoes.
Out of those holes
run all my summertime
blues.

Dance with me, dance!